I NEED A WEE!

For our Alan, with love
Sue Hendra & Paul Linnet

I NEED A WEE!
SIMON AND SCHUSTER
London • New York
Sydney • Toronto • New Delhi

Alan the bear loved whizzing down the helter-skelter with his friends.

WAHOOO! WHEEEEE!

It was SO MUCH FUN!

"Let's go on again!" said Alan.

"Alan, why are you dancing?" asked Giraffe.

"I'm not dancing!" said Alan. "I need a wee! But first I need just one more go."

"No," said Giraffe. "When you've got to go, you've got to go."

But getting Alan to the toilets wasn't going to be easy.

"Ooooh, just one balloon!" he cried.

"Alan, come on, before it's too late," said Giraffe.

Then Alan saw Claude's party.

"Ooooh, just one piece of cake!" he cried.

"No time!" said Robot.

Finally they got there.

“Oh dear,” said Giraffe. “Can you hold on?
It’s going to be a long wait.”

“But I can’t wait,” said Alan . . .

"I NEED A WEE!"

"Don't worry!" called a little dolly.
"I can help. You can come to my house!"

"PHEW!" said the friends.

"Oh no! I can't wee in there," said Alan.
"It's a teeny tiny toilet!"

And off he went.

“No! You can’t wee in there!” whispered Robot.
“It’s a teapot – not a wee-pot!”

"How about this hat?" said Alan. "It's perfect."

And he was just about to
have a wee when . . .

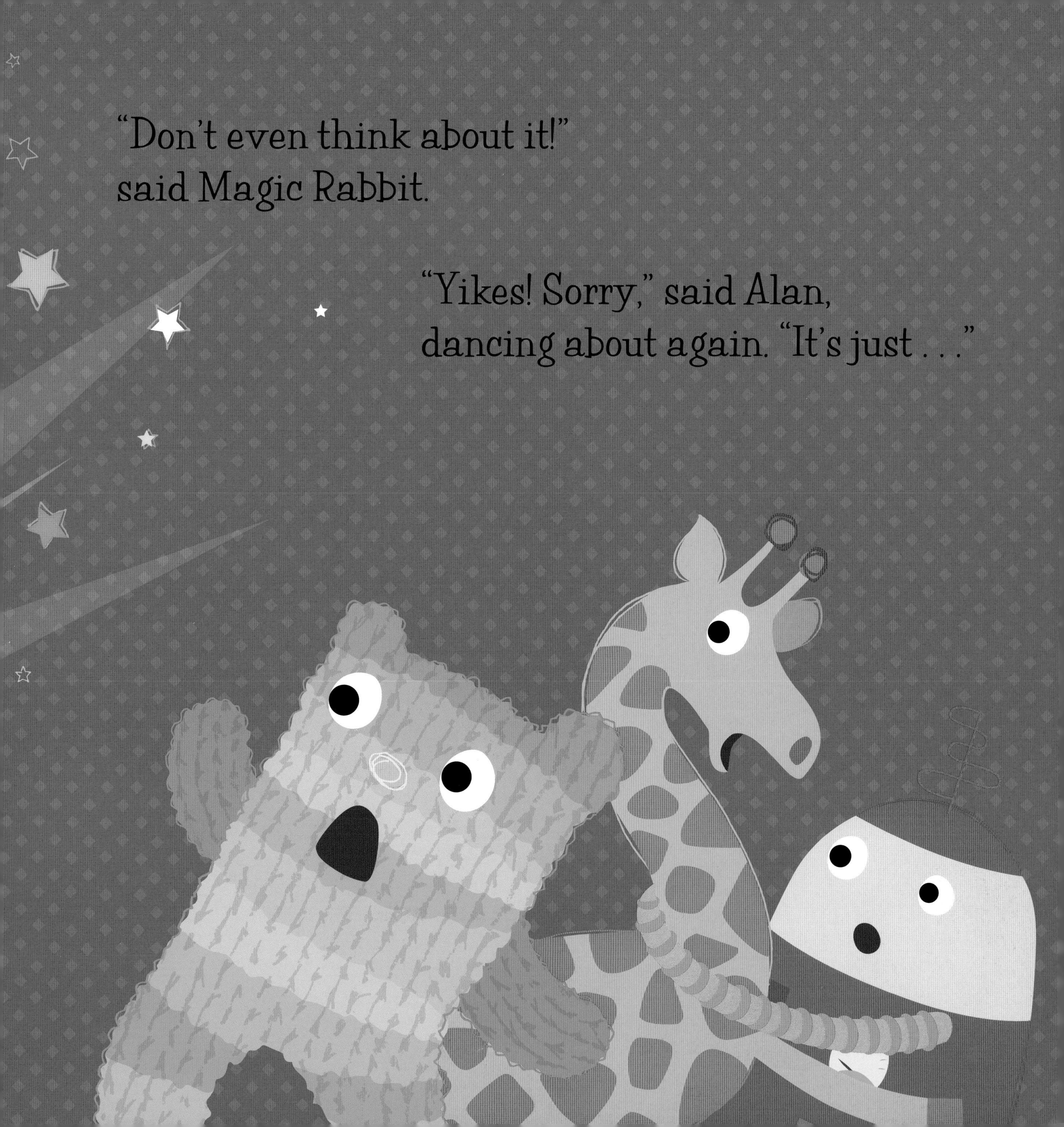

"Don't even think about it!"
said Magic Rabbit.

"Yikes! Sorry," said Alan,
dancing about again. "It's just . . ."

"I NEED A WEE!"

By now things were getting desperate.

"Quick, behind that curtain!" shouted Robot.

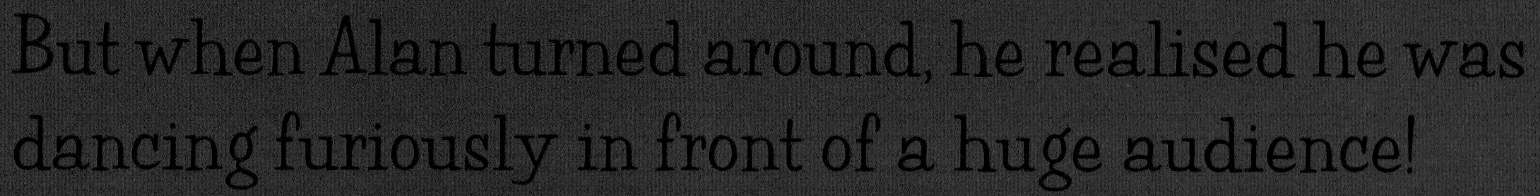

But when Alan turned around, he realised he was dancing furiously in front of a huge audience!

The crowd whooped. They cheered.
They'd never seen dancing like it!

"And the winner of the international toy dancing competition is . . ."

"Alan, my name's Alan."

"And how do you feel to have won the cup, Alan?"

"Ahhhhh!" said Alan at last.
"I feel fantastic!"

"Well, what a relief," said Robot, smiling. "Thank goodness you don't need a wee any more."

"Oh no, I definitely do!" grinned Alan.

WHEEEEEEE!

The End?

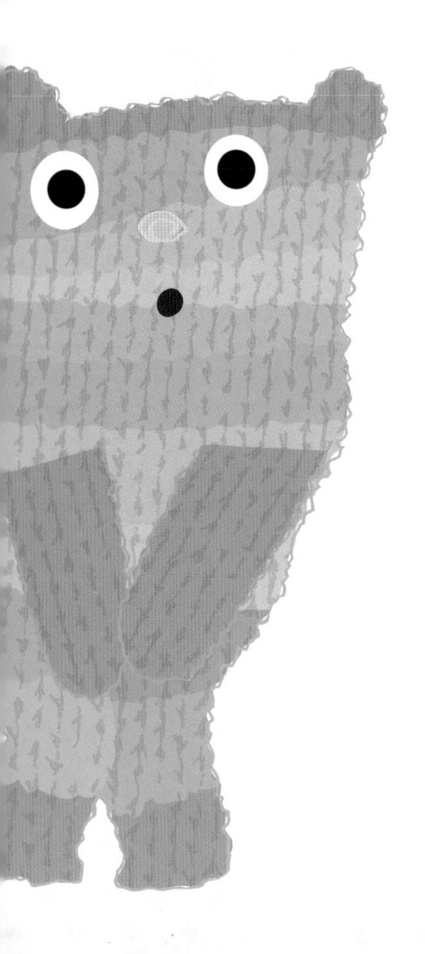

SIMON AND SCHUSTER
First published in Great Britain in 2015
by Simon and Schuster UK Ltd
1st Floor, 222 Gray's Inn Road, London, WC1X 8HB
A CBS Company

A CIP catalogue record for this book is available
from the British Library upon request

978-1-4711-2088-6 (HB)
978-1-4711-6348-7 (PB)
978-1-4711-2089-3 (eBook)

Printed in China
3 5 7 9 10 8 6 4 2